POOR JACK

Jack

POOR JACK

is for his number one fans,
Robert, Matthew, Cormac, Gerald
and Joseph Power.
And Judith Murdoch.

POOR Jack

Una Power

Illustrated by
Sonia Holleyman

ORCHARD BOOKS

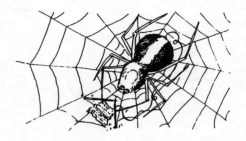

ORCHARD BOOKS
96 Leonard Street, London EC2A 4RH

Orchard Books Australia
14 Mars Road, Lane Cove, NSW 2066
ISBN 1 85213 519 0 (paperback)
ISBN 1 85213 244 2 (hardback)

Printed and bound in Great Britain
A CIP catalogue record for this book is available from the British Library.

Contents

Chapter 1

Jack's Birthday

Jack Allgood had had a very happy childhood growing up on his father's island. His parents loved him dearly and would have bought him anything he wanted, for they were very, very rich. But Jack was not greedy or spoilt, and only wanted his parents' love. Everything was wonderful until Jack's mother died and his Aunt Selina came to live with them.

Allgood House was the only house on the island. It was surrounded by tall trees with great leafy branches, green lawns, and white sandy beaches. Hares leapt across pathways and disappeared into dense undergrowth. Rabbits hopped about in the vegetable garden when nobody was looking, nibbling at the lettuces and carrots. Occasionally Jack caught sight of a graceful deer in the woods near the house. Robins, sparrows, red and yellow finches and many other birds were all quite at home on the island. Once, when Jack was up and out of doors early in the morning, he had spotted a long-legged heron by the edge of the lake in front of Allgood House, but it had been frightened off by the sound of the crows nesting in the nearby trees.

Best of all Jack liked the big brilliantly coloured butterflies that settled on the leaves of the bushes. Some were a glorious shade of blue, others red and black, and very rarely, there were green butterflies. There were white butterflies in abundance.

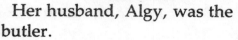

"They are called Cabbage Whites," Maud Biffen told him. Maud was the Allgoods' housekeeper.

Her husband, Algy, was the butler.

They lived with them and were very kind to Jack. "At least, that's what they were called in my young days, for they like nothing better than eating cabbage leaves."

Maud and Algy had worked in the Allgood home for years and loved the family very much. Sometimes Maud pretended to be cross. She

8

would say:

"You're a funny family. You're just like gypsies – happier eating a picnic in the woods, or scrambling down the cliff to the beach to eat bread and cheese, than sitting in that lovely big dining room like civilised folk."

One day, on Jack's seventh birthday, his father had a surprise for him.

"We're not having a birthday party in the house, Jack. We're going out in the boat to catch some fish. When we have caught them we'll cook them on the beach."

"That sounds great," said Jack. "Is Mum coming too?"

"Just try leaving Mum behind! I love an adventure," said Jack's mother; and laughing and joking they all set off for the beach.

Even though it was a bright summer day with the bushes loaded with red and green berries, they took crumbs for the birds. There was a big lake in front of the house and the family stopped there to throw the crumbs around and watch as first one then another bird hopped towards them to peck up the bread.

To Jack's surprise they did not take the usual path to the beach. Instead Jack's father led them through the wood and to some bushes at the edge of a part of the cliffs where no one ever came. Jack was puzzled.

"Have you changed your mind about going down to the beach?" he asked his father.

"No. But I want to show you a secret that I've known about for years."

"A secret!" said Jack excitedly. Jack's father parted the bushes and pointed downwards. Stepping forward Jack looked curiously to where his father was pointing and saw a narrow path, cut like deep steps, leading straight down to the beach. "It's a secret pathway!"

"That's right, Jack. The Allgood secret pathway to the beach. When my brother Cyril and I were your age, our father showed us this path. Now it's your secret path. What do you think?"

"I think it's the nicest birthday present I have ever had."

"That's not all. When we get to the beach there is another secret I want to show you."

Jack could hardly wait to explore his secret path and scrambled down quickly. When he got to the beach he looked around. He could not imagine what other secret there could be down there. It was a part of the beach that Jack rarely used. He had only been here a couple of times before. Waves lapped against the sand carrying little bits of wood and seaweed. Gulls flew about screeching and calling to each other. The cliff rose up from the sand: there were a couple of boulders lying against the cliff, but nothing else. Jack felt a bit disappointed, and told his mother so when his parents joined him.

"Why don't you go and look behind that big boulder over there?" suggested his mother.

"I know what the secret is! You've hidden a present behind the boulder," shouted Jack as he ran across the sand.

But there was no present to be seen behind the
boulder. Instead Jack saw a great yawning opening in the cliff. It was the entrance to a cave!

"That's funny," said Jack. "I never knew there
was a cave here!" He was so
excited he could
hardly speak.

"That's because I moved
another boulder to shield
the spot. It's the Allgood Secret
Cave. Now it's yours, Jack.
Here, take this torch – it'll be
dark inside." Jack's father gave
him a little shove. "Go on in and explore."

Shining the torch around, Jack saw that a stone ledge ran around it just like a seat. There were some boxes, coils of rope, a frying pan, a saucepan and a primus stove on the floor.

"The cave is *huge*," breathed Jack. "I can hardly see to the back of it. And it's *mine*, my own secret cave. This is a smashing present. Thanks, Dad."

"There is something else," said Jack's mother, giving him a hug and a kiss. "Would you like to open that parcel on the floor?"

Jack had been too excited to notice the parcel. It was a square shape and wrapped in shiny gold paper. Carrying it outside, he tore off the wrapping and saw to his delight that it was a book about dinosaurs. Jack loved dinosaurs. His mother had been showing him how to collect bits of wood and material to make dinosaur models. Already he had quite a collection. In the book there were pictures of large, hideous-looking animals with gigantic scales, sharp claws and massive teeth and jaws.

13

"They are like the alligators that Great Aunt Marigold used to photograph in the Amazon," Jack said to his father.

Mr Allgood smiled. "Poor old Aunt Marigold. The last we heard she was wrestling with an alligator that swallowed her camera. He probably swallowed her too."

"I doubt that, somehow," said Jack's mother. "She is a very tough old lady. Don't you remember that time when a maddened elephant was charging through the jungle? He was just about to trample a village down when Aunt Marigold flung herself in his path and knocked him down with that big stick she always carried. She saved the village, but her best panama hat got a bit battered."

Jack loved hearing stories about his Great Aunt Marigold. She sounded more interesting than anyone else in the world.

Presently they all went along to the place where they kept their fishing boat. All the way along the beach Jack kept giving skips of pure joy as he clutched his new dinosaur book and thought how lucky he was to have a secret path, a secret cave and the most wonderful parents in the world.

It wasn't long before they were bobbing about on the waves with Jack holding the fishing rod over the side of the boat.

"I've caught something! I can feel a tug on the line. It's something really big." Jack was pleased with himself.

Jack and his mother reeled in the biggest fish Jack had ever seen while his father shipped oars and smiled at him in admiration.

"We're going to have a real birthday feast with that one," he said.

Back on the beach they lit a fire and cooked the fish. After they finished eating they all said it was the best meal they had had for a long time.

"Hunger is a great sauce," said Jack's father. "Always remember, Jack, that no matter how rich you are and no matter how many people you have to wait on you, the things that you can do for yourself are always the nicest. It's much better to be independent."

They scrambled back up Jack's secret path and went into the house where Algy and Maud Biffen were waiting for them.

"Maud has made a very nice birthday cake for Jack," said Algy Biffen. "Would you like me to serve it in the dining room?"

"No, we're much too dirty," said Jack's mother. "We'll all come down to the kitchen and eat there."

There was a big birthday cake with yellow icing and seven candles. Jack's parents and the Biffens all sang "Happy Birthday to You", at the tops of their voices.

"This is the happiest day of my life," Jack told them all.

"Blow out your candles, love, and make a wish," Jack's mother told him.

Closing his eyes and blowing very hard, Jack managed to blow out all his candles in one go.

"I wish next year I have a birthday just like this one."

But Jack's wish never came true. A week before his eighth birthday, on a lovely summer morning, his mother died.

Chapter 2

Aunt Selina Comes to Stay

Everyone was very sad after Mrs Allgood died.
The Biffens did their best to make nice meals but
no one had much appetite for food. Jack felt as
though a light had gone out in his world. Then
one day his father came to him out by the lake
where he was sailing a model boat. He was holding a letter in his hand.

"I have some good news, Jack. Your Aunt
Selina is coming to stay with her four children.
She has agreed to live here and look after
things."

Jack pulled the model boat in by a piece of
string.

"I can't remember my Aunt Selina. Is she
nice?"

"She is one of the most beautiful people in the
world. She was married to my brother Cyril and
after Cyril died she went to live in a big city. Now

she says she would love to live on the island and look after you. Isn't that kind of her? And just think! You'll have two little boys and two little girls to play with."

Jack thought it was a wonderful idea and could hardly wait for the day to arrive when his Aunt Selina and his four cousins would come to the island.

Then Jack's father got another letter; this time it said that he must go and attend to some very urgent business on the other side of the world. Jack's father was a very rich and important business man; sometimes he had to go away for weeks at a time.

"What a shame! I won't be here when Aunt Selina arrives. You will have to make her and her four children, Jason, Wayne, Marlene and Sharon, very welcome. And promise me that you will do everything that your Aunt Selina tells you."

Jack's father kept a few aeroplanes parked on the runway at the back of the house. He climbed into one of the machines and waving goodbye to Jack, he took off.

Jack occupied himself helping Maud and Algy Biffen get the rooms ready for Aunt Selina and the children. They cleaned, dusted and polished until the five rooms sparkled. Then they put bunches of flowers in each room. Jack picked them himself. He had gone out early to get blue speedwell, yellow sunflowers, white daisies, red carnations and orange marigolds. The flowers looked and smelled lovely. It took him a long time because he stopped to watch a spider weaving a web.

Every evening Jack and the Biffens would sit in the kitchen eating chocolate digestive biscuits and drinking cocoa.

"You'd better get to bed early tonight, Jack. Your Aunt Selina will be here on the supply ferry in the morning. I'll give you an early call," Maud Biffen told him.

But Jack didn't need an early call; he was up and dressed soon after dawn. Then he went down to the landing stage to wait for the ferry. He knew he was much too early but he was too excited to stay in the house or concentrate on anything else. The ferry came to island every third Friday with supplies; food, cleaning materials and all the things a house needs. When they needed clothes, the family usually flew off in one of the Allgood planes to somewhere where there were a lot of shops.

The postman came once a week with letters and parcels. As there was never any post for him Jack wasn't much interested in the postman, but the ferryman was different. The ferryman let Jack

19

help him unload the boat. Then they would have a teabreak and the ferryman would give Jack his wages. It made Jack feel important. Jack's father would come down to the kitchen and ask how the workers were. That made him feel even more important.

Even though it was August and the sun ought to have been shining, it was a dull, cloudy day and the ferry, when Jack first sighted it, was surrounded by mist. As it drew closer and closer to the landing stage Jack began to dance from foot to foot, he was so excited. The ferry drew alongside the landing stage and a crewman jumped out and tied up the boat. Then he turned to help a woman ashore.

Jack thought she was almost as beautiful as his mother and ran forward to meet her.

Aunt Selina

"Hello. You must be my Aunt Selina." He held out his hand to shake hands. "I'm Jack."

Aunt Selina shook hands with him, patted his head and turned to the crewman who had helped her.

"Be very careful with all my possessions. They are very important and valuable and I don't want anything dropped or broken by you idiots. See that big box over there?" She pointed to a large crate. "That contains all my wigs. I don't want anything to happen to it."

"Righty ho, ducky."

"Ducky? Kindly call me madam."

Jack was surprised at this. He had never heard his parents speak in that haughty tone of voice.

They were always the same, no matter to whom they were speaking. He felt a bit disappointed already, but he had promised his father he would be welcoming to his aunt and her children. He looked around and saw a girl of twelve or so coming ashore.

"That's Marlene," said Aunt Selina. "Isn't she pretty?"

Jack didn't think someone who stuck her nose in the air and looked at him as though he were a cockroach was pretty at all, but he was much too polite to say so.

Then came another girl of about eleven. She was not looking at Jack. Instead, she was poking out her tongue at the ferryman. Jack was very surprised at this; the ferryman was one of his favourite people.

"That's my little Sharon," said Aunt Selina. "She's the sweetest little thing, isn't she?"

Then Aunt Selina's smile became even more fond as she called out, "Where's Jason? Jason, my angel, come and meet your cousin Jack."

Jason emerged from behind the wig crate. His tee-shirt was smeared with chocolate and his hair was standing on end.

"I don't want to meet my cousin Jack. Where are the shops? I want to buy some more chocolate."

"Hello, Jason. I'm afraid there aren't any shops here."

"No shops? What kind of dump is this place?"

That made Jack angry. He loved his island. But once, when he had got angry before, his father had told him very seriously: "If you've the need to be angry you've no right, and if you've the right to be angry, you've no need." He hadn't really understood what it meant at the time. But looking at Jason's ugly sneer, he did understand.

"Don't worry, Jason. I bet you'll come to love it all as much as I do."

"I doubt it. Got a telly?"

"Of course he's got a telly. There is probably one in every room. They are rolling in money, aren't you, Jack? Anyway we'll talk about it later. I want you to meet my baby, my little Wayne." Marlene, Sharon and Jason all exchanged looks of disgust.

Jack waited for a baby in arms to be carried ashore. "Where is Wayne?" called Aunt Selina. "Come along, darling."

"If he is a baby, shouldn't he be carried ashore?" Jack asked.

"He's not a baby," Jason said, or rather snarled. "He's her pet, and he's always running to her with tales that she's stupid enough to believe. That's why I thumped him."

This shocked Jack very much; but what shocked him more was the way he had spoken about his mother. Not that she noticed, for she had a foolish smile on her face. Her arms were outstretched to a boy of about nine. Suddenly Jack longed for his own mother. If only Aunt Selina could come to love him as much as she loved her own children, life might be all right again.

"Here's my baby. Here's my Wayne." Aunt Selina's voice was soft and loving.

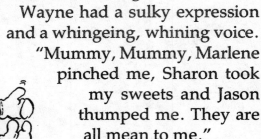

Wayne had a sulky expression and a whingeing, whining voice. "Mummy, Mummy, Marlene pinched me, Sharon took my sweets and Jason thumped me. They are all mean to me."

Aunt Selina swept him up into her arms and cuddled him.

The poor treasure was making faces at his brother and sisters over his mother's shoulder. Jack wondered if he could ever come to like Wayne. Then he remembered that his father had said that he must welcome all his cousins, and he sighed. For a moment he felt like joining his cousins who were making faces back at Wayne. But he was well-mannered, although he felt that good manners could be a bit of a curse at times.

After a lot of squabbling, shouting, and tearing around, the family eventually got settled in.

"Who put cissy flowers in my room?" shrieked Jason. "Hey, you!" he shouted at Maud Biffen. "Get them out of my room."

"If you don't like them, Jason, you take them out yourself."

"That's *your* job, you're supposed to be a servant, aren't you?"

Jack didn't like that one little bit.

"Don't speak to Maud Biffen like that, Jason. It isn't allowed."

"Oh, yeah? Who says?"

Jack was small for his age but he was full of courage. Once he had had to climb up a very big tree to rescue a kitten that was stuck in the top branch. Now he faced Jason and looked him straight in the eye.

"Maud and Algy Biffen are our friends. When my father returns he will be very angry if he hears that you have treated his friends in that way."

"Oh, yeah, and who'll tell him?"

Aunt Selina had been listening to all this and when she heard that Mr Allgood might not like the way they were behaving to Maud and Algy she looked a bit uneasy.

"Children! I want you all to be very polite to the Biffens."

They tried really hard for about an hour, but they couldn't keep up good behaviour for long; it just wasn't natural to them. The Biffens had made a delicious meat and vegetable stew, with a mountain of potatoes and a dish of peas.

"Brilliant," said Jack, who was very hungry.

"I'm not eating this garbage," snarled Jason. "I want chips with curry sauce."

"I want a beefburger with onions," yelled Wayne, "I want a beefburger, I want a beefburger, I want a beefburger." He was becoming hysterical. Aunt Selina looked alarmed.

"I think you'd better take the stew away, Mrs Biffen, and bring the children some proper food. And bring me a very large gin and tonic."

"I want ice cream for my dinner," Marlene said.

"If she's having ice cream I want some too, but more than her," said Sharon.

"Yes, give her more, then she'll have twice as many spots," said Marlene spitefully.

This made Sharon hit Marlene with her spoon; in return Marlene poured salt down the back of Sharon's dress. Jason and Wayne started guffawing with horrible laughter. Jack felt as if he were in a madhouse.

"The darlings," said Aunt Selina, lighting a cigarette, "they are so high-spirited."

When Maud and Algy took the dishes away, Jack slipped out after them, and leaving his relations to shriek and yell themselves hoarse, went down to the kitchen to eat his dinner in peace.

CHAPTER 3

Sad News for Jack

Aunt Selina and her children had been at Allgood House for a month, making everyone's life hell, when there was a telephone call. Algy Biffen answered the telephone. His face was very serious. He called Maud to him and they both cried. Jack wondered what could be wrong.

"Your father has been killed in a plane accident, Jack," Maud told him, tears running down her face. "I am so sorry, my poor child, we are all going to miss him very much."

Jack felt cold and sad. It was strange and lonely when his mother died, but his father had been there, strong and loving. Now he was all alone. There was nobody except the Biffens, and although he loved them very much, they were not his own parents. Aunt Selina and her children were unkind and unpleasant – Jack knew that he did not love them. It was because his father had asked him to be polite and welcoming to the family that he bothered at all. If it hadn't been for that, Jack would have told Aunt Selina and Jason, Wayne, Marlene and Sharon exactly what he thought of them, which wasn't much.

Even Aunt Selina and her children were shocked and quiet when they heard the terrible news about Jack's father.

"We must send for the solicitor and find out how much I get in the will," said Aunt Selina briskly.

"What's a will?" Jack asked Algy Biffen.

"It's a letter that a person writes, so that after they are dead everyone knows what their wishes are."

All the following week Aunt Selina spoke to grave-faced men in the library. The children were not allowed in. They were all curious but no one would tell them anything. Eventually the grave-faced men – solicitors, Aunt Selina told them – left and she called the children and the Biffens into the library.

She looked very angry.

"The solicitors have told me that Jack's father left him *everything* – it's disgraceful! What can a little toad like Jack want with millions and millions of pounds, fleets of oil tankers, oil wells, sailing ships, houses all over the world and this island!"

"Don't *you* get anything?" Jason shouted.

"Only a measly million pounds. *And* to get that I've got to promise to stay on here and look after Jack and all his affairs, and even to hire a school-teacher to have you all taught lessons here on the island."

"I'm not staying on this boring island, I hate it!" Marlene stamped her foot.

"There are no shops," wailed Sharon. "What do we do if we want new clothes?"

"We have to go to the mainland every so often. Though how long a million pounds will last, I just don't know. The price of gin is going up all the time." Aunt Selina looked furiously at Jack as though everything was his fault.

"A million pounds is a lot of money, and surely, you have an allowance to pay all the expenses of the house," said Algy Biffen quietly.

"Huh! I wanted money for myself and for my own dear children." Aunt Selina tapped her foot and lit a cigarette. She looked at Jack with hate-filled eyes. "The only way *I* get the money is if Jack dies. He is so small and puny that he might have an accident. Or he might be ill and not recover." She was so upset that she was beginning to rant and rave, although Jack did not realise this.

"*We* shall make sure that Jack is all right and nothing happens to him," Maud spoke up.

"Yes, you would, wouldn't you?" snapped Aunt Selina. "You get a tidy little sum in the will and you don't even have to stay on this lousy island if you don't want to."

"We're staying to look after Jack."

The Biffens spoke together.

"You're staying just as long as *I* say you can stay. Jack's father left me in charge of everything. So just watch your step!" Aunt Selina warned them.

Jack was glad that he was to stay in his own home on the island; it would have broken his heart to have had to leave. He did not like his

Aunt Selina or her children, but at least the Biffens were to stay. That thought comforted him.

"Our favourite game," Jason told Jack, "is shutting little boys into cupboards and frightening them."

"Please, don't shut me in a cupboard. I'd hate that."

This made his cousins grin. They were supposed to be doing some quiet reading and were bored.

When they put Jack in the cupboard he cried and they laughed.

Hours later Aunt Selina found him crying in the cupboard and was very surprised.

"My cousins shut me in here. It was terrible and dark and I've been very frightened."

"Don't tell such terrible lies, Jack! My children are good and kind and sweet-natured. They would never do a thing like that. I expect you like being in cupboards and only went in there to escape having to do your reading. Thank goodness I have arranged to have a teacher start working here next week. He is an old friend of mine and will live in the house. I shall turn that big room on the first floor into a schoolroom."

"Do you mean my bedroom?" Jack felt very upset. He loved his room.

"Yes, it's the only one that's suitable. Besides

it's much too big for you. Now that you have in-herited all the money you will only get a big head and be a bad influence on my children. You'll have to go and live in the attic. It will be good for you and I shan't have to see you."

"If only you could love me, Aunt Selina!" poor Jack cried out desperately.

"Love a little shrimp like you? I can hardly bear to look at you. Go on, get packed up and get up to the attic. Get the Biffens to help you. They seem to love you, even though they know you are a lazy trouble-maker."

When Jack went down to the kitchen and told the Biffens about living in the attic, they were furious.

"It's a disgrace, a living disgrace!" said Maud. "This is a great big luxurious house with fitted carpets you'd sink into and she wants to put the little mite into that cold dreary attic. She must be a madwoman."

Algy shook his head sadly. "No one has been in that attic in living memory. They won't go near it because there are rats up there. Don't you worry, Jack. I'm going straight up to tell her that we won't allow her to put you in the attic."

But Aunt Selina sacked them that very day and hired a new butler and housekeeper.

The butler, George Pomfret, was a fat, stupid man and the housekeeper, Hester Wallow, was a thin, spiteful woman. They had both worked for Aunt Selina for years and were devoted to her.

Jack had thought that life was sad enough. He missed his parents very much and knew that he would miss the Biffens. He didn't think, in his wildest imaginings, that things could get worse. But the moment the new butler and housekeeper stepped into Allgood House, poor Jack's misery really began.

Chapter 4

Jack Gets the Blame

Jack decided that he quite liked his attic. It was cold, but he soon made it comfortable. There was a small iron bed with a blanket, a closet in which he kept his clothes and a big table where he made things. Jack was quite an expert modelmaker. He had spent hours on the beach and in the woods with his mother collecting leaves, stones, wood and seaweed to make the models, and they were very realistic. In a way he was pleased to be in the attic. At least no one ever came up there; he had begun to get fed up with the way the children came into his room and took his toys and books. They had not seen his dinosaur book and he had no intention of letting them see it. They would probably rip it up.

As soon as he made his bed and swept his attic he went down to breakfast. His cousins were at their usual breakfast-time carry-on. Jason

amused himself by flinging bits of toast at Marlene. Marlene was wearing one of her best skirts and jumpers and had done her hair differently, plaited at the back of her head. She was due to have a birthday party in a couple of weeks' time, at the end of September.
She was always trying
out different hair styles,
to impress everyone.
Standing in front of the
mirror over the fireplace
she turned her head this
way and that watching
her reflection. By the
expression on her face she
was obviously thinking
that she was incredibly
lovely. A bit of toast landed on her head and she screeched at Jason.

"You dirty lout. You aren't fit to live with a pig!"

"No, but you are!" said Jason, grinning.

When Sharon wasn't looking Wayne put a handful of sugar on her eggs and bacon and laughed at the expression on her face when she took a mouthful.

Their mother looked at them all with a foolish doting smile on her face. Their carry-on, she said, was because they were all so brainy and creative. But when Jack came into the room she frowned at him.

"You're late, Jack." That was not true. "Don't expect to sit there making a beast of yourself over eggs and bacon when you can't be bothered to come down in time. Go down to the kitchen and ask the butler for another pot of coffee, this lot's cold," she snapped, stubbing out her cigarette in her saucer.

Jack decided that it wasn't worth arguing with her and went down to the kitchen.

George Pomfret and Hester Wallow were sitting at the kitchen table eating eggs and bacon.

It puzzled Jack that in the beginning the butler and housekeeper had seemed to like him. Now they were always hostile. What he didn't know was that his Aunt Selina had called the servants to come to her one morning soon after they arrived and told them:

"If that little rat, Jack, were dead, I would inherit all the money. If I had plenty of money I would give you some."

"Are you asking us to kill Jack?" demanded Hester Wallow.

"All I'm saying at this stage is, let's not be too careful about keeping him alive. Drop the odd brick on his head. Try tripping him up when he's going up the stairs. If there are any rotten vegetables or bad eggs, give them to Jack."

"We'll do it, but we're not taking any blame," said George Pomfret.

Now Jack looked at them both. "My aunt wants some more coffee," he told Hester Wallow.

Hester Wallow was chewing on a piece of bacon rind. "Is that true?" she demanded sharply. "I believe you are a boy who tells lies. Are you sure you don't want it for yourself?"

George Pomfret stared at Jack. "He is probably telling lies. Remember Mrs Allgood said he was a liar and a trouble-maker. See that lovely big chocolate cake you have just made, Hester?" He

pointed to the dresser where a great big chocolate cake with cream and icing lay. "He probably came here to steal it. If you don't clear off, I'll lock you in the cupboard under the stairs."

Turning his fat back on Jack he picked up a fried egg in his fingers and stuffed it into his mouth. The yellow yolk ran down his chin.

"Now look at the mess I'm in," he said angrily. "It's all your fault, Jack. Get out!"

egg YOLK ON Chin

Jack decided to play a trick on the mean butler and housekeeper. Instead of going up to the dining room, he went into a room that lay at the back of the old range. In the old days the room at the back of the kitchen had been used for storing food; but now that there were refrigerators, the room was not used. Algy Biffen had shown him a trick that Jack's father used to play. If a person went in to the disused room and spoke into the empty fireplace, the sound carried, very eerily, into the old chimney in the kitchen range. And the best part of it was that the person in the kitchen could not tell where the eerie sound came from. Usually they thought they were being haunted by a ghost.

Kneeling down by the empty fireplace, Jack called out in a frightening voice: "George Pomfret, Hester Wallow. I am watching you. I am coming to get you."

When he went back to the kitchen he laughed when he saw it was empty. His trick had worked. He went to the window and laughed again when he saw the butler's fat body heaving and wobbling as he tried to run across the lawn after Hester Wallow. The housekeeper's skinny legs were like dark matchsticks flying across the lawn.

They both looked scared to death.

Then Jack cooked himself a very good breakfast. After putting sausages into the frying pan, he opened a tin of beans and heated them in a saucepan. Jack was a good cook and never burned anything. Jason told Jack that cooking was nonsense and that any boy who could cook must be a cissy, which just showed what a fool Jason was.

George Pomfret and Hester Wallow wouldn't go back into the kitchen for ages.

"We're terrified, madam," Hester told Aunt Selina. "The place is riddled with ghosts out to get George and me." Hester Wallow really did look frightened.

"I don't care about that." Aunt Selina was cross. "If I don't get my dinner, *I'll* be out to get you. So just get yourselves into the kitchen and get my dinner – or else!"

The butler and the housekeeper didn't wait to find out what the "or else" might be, they crept into the kitchen in a very quiet mood. Every so often they looked fearfully over their shoulders, and every time there was a noise they jumped nervously.

No one suspected that Jack had played a trick; they all really thought that there was a ghost in the house. That made Jack laugh.

Chapter 5

Jack Saves a Life

The new schoolteacher, Ernest Croachbody, had arrived a week earlier. He was a tall bony man with large, yellowish teeth, small black eyes and bristling black eyebrows. He boasted that he had been in the army and had been very heroic. His job had been to stay in the general's office with a large fly-swatter, keeping flies away from the general's heroic head.

"There were armies of them," he recalled, his little eyes gleaming with the memory of his days of glory. "But I beat them off, I held them at bay so that the general could get on with his work of saving the country."

He was ridiculously proud of the medal he had earned when he left the army. It was a miniature brass fly-swatter with a coloured ribbon dangling from it.

"Earned the hard way, in the course of duty,"

he said in a proud growling voice.

Aunt Selina, unknown to Jack, had also told Ernest Croachbody that she wanted to kill Jack and that if he helped her he would get a large sum of money. When Jack came into the room after playing the trick on the butler and housekeeper, Ernest Croachbody glared at him ferociously, and sent him to a desk in the corner of the room, farthest from the fire.

"Why are you in first?" he demanded. "Are you trying to get into my good books? It won't work. Your aunt has warned me over and over about you. I am going to watch you very carefully, Jack Allgood. You can't read or write nearly as well as your cousins."

"That's not fair, Mr Croachbody. They are all older than me. Marlene is nearly thirteen, Sharon is eleven and Jason is ten. Even Wayne is a year older than me. They have been having lessons for far longer than me. I like my lessons, and *I* think I'm quite good at them." Jack was fed up at the way everyone was getting at him.

"Stop being cheeky! If there is one thing I cannot bear it is an uncivil, insubordinate child. When I was in the army, it wasn't tolerated." He began walking back and forth, clasping his big bony hands behind his back, sticking his long chin forward. "As to the little matter of your

47

believing that you are good at your lessons, I can only say that it sounds to me as though you are a boastful, bragging child. As punishment, fetch the telephone directory and copy out all the names, addresses and telephone numbers by the end of the week."

Jack gasped. "But there must be thousands of names in the telephone directory!"

The teacher smiled unpleasantly. "If you are as clever as you say you are, Jack, that won't be a problem, will it?" Rubbing his hands together, Ernest Croachbody's unpleasant smile widened, so that Jack could see all his yellowish teeth. "Bring me the work on Friday, or I shall have a very nasty punishment for you."

As Jack was going out of the schoolroom he met his cousins. He told them all about Mr Croachbody's unreasonable demand.

"I could do it if you helped me," he said.

Jason, Wayne, Marlene and Sharon exchanged sly, crafty looks. They were always looking for a way to escape having to go to their lessons.

"We'll help, Jack, if you come with us on to the lake and row the boat," said Marlene.

Jack agreed. Although it was difficult to row the boat with all of them in it, he somehow managed. He was small for his age, but he was very strong and full of courage.

"This is better than going up to old Croachbody for lessons," said Jason.

Jason took a bar of chocolate out of his pocket and with a stupid cocky smile at Wayne unwrapped it and started to eat it. Wayne stood up and tried to snatch the chocolate from his brother, over-balanced and fell into the water.

Jack knew that there is one golden rule if you get into difficulties in water – DON'T PANIC. When he saw Wayne toppling over he had reached out a hand to try to save him, but he was too late. Now he held out an oar for Wayne to hold on to.

"Take the oar, Wayne. Hold on to it, paddle your feet in the water and I'll help you into the boat."

Marlene and Sharon started to scream, not because their brother was in the water and couldn't swim, but because they could see their mother walking across the lawn with Ernest Croachbody. The expression on her face was ugly and angry.

Jack didn't have time to notice this because he was too busy saving Wayne's life.

Once Wayne was safely back in the boat, Jack started rowing back to the edge of the lake. He smiled hopefully when he saw his aunt. Perhaps they will begin to like me now that I have rescued Wayne, he thought.

But as the reached the bank, his aunt grabbed him by the hair and dragged him from the boat.

"You little viper!" she screeched. "I saw you push your cousin into the water and try to drown him with an oar. That's the gratitude you show for the sacrifice we make to stay here and care for your lousy little person. Get up to the attic and stay there." She pushed Jack away from her and turned to her children with tears in her eyes. "Come into the house, my poor children, and have some nice chocolate cake, and I'll have a gin and tonic. We've all had the most terrible shock."

Jack was disappointed and annoyed. "That's not fair, Aunt Selina. They made me go. When Wayne fell in to the water, *I* saved his life."

"My children would not do such a thing, would you, my darlings?"

The darlings all looked innocent and sadly shook their heads.

Wayne put on a whining voice, a thing he always did when he was in trouble. "I wouldn't do anything naughty, Mummy, honestly, I wouldn't. I was so frightened because I couldn't swim."

"That's not my fault, Aunt Selina," said Jack. "All children should learn to swim."

This made Aunt Selina look thoughtful. Marlene couldn't bear to think that Jack might come up with a good suggestion so she interrupted quickly.

"It was all Jack's idea. He wanted us to help him with some work Mr Croachbody gave him. We

51

promised we would, but when he said he was going out in the boat we were afraid something might happen to him, so we thought we had better go with him and make sure he was all right," Marlene lied.

Aunt Selina's eyes filled with tears as she looked at Marlene. "What did I do to deserve such beautiful, noble children?"

Ernest Croachbody looked like a large wolf about to devour a lamb; rubbing his hands together, he spoke mournfully. "All this is too true. Jack is a lazy wicked boy. I can do nothing with him."

"Then there is no point in his having lessons with my children. He is a bad influence. From now on, Jack, you can stay in your attic and do whatever work Mr Croachbody is kind enough to set you, up there."

George Pomfret had been holding open the big front door of Allgood House and he heard Mrs Allgood say that her children were to have the chocolate cake. This frightened him because he had just eaten all the cake. Wiping the crumbs from his mouth and chin with a big fat hand, he decided that he would put the blame on Jack, and say that he had eaten the cake.

As the family trooped through the big front door and went into the drawing room he tried to shut the door on Jack and squash him. As soon as he saw Jack going upstairs, he went into the drawing room after the family.

He put a pained expression on his big moon face. He looked as though someone had stuck a pin into him.

"There is no cake. Jack stole it and ate it all."

The children started screaming hysterically, lying on the carpet, drumming their heels, banging their fists, lashing themselves into a fury.

"Jack is a greedy pig!" His aunt was furious. "From now on, he can have leftover scraps from the table sent up to his attic. That will teach him not to steal cake!"

Hester Wallow was angry with Jack because she believed George Pomfret's lies. But she pretended to be nice to him. She went up to his attic.

"I'm sorry that you have to stay in the attic, Jack. Don't worry, I'll look after you and give you some nice little treats. Would you like some more cake? I know you are fond of chocolate cake?"

"I didn't eat the cake, but, yes, I would like some, if it's not too much trouble."

"It will be a pleasure, Jack."

"It will be a pleasure"

Cruel Hester Wallow made a cake from all the nastiest things she could find in the kitchen. She mixed rotten eggs, stale flour and rancid butter in a bowl. Then she went to a locked cupboard. Opening it, she took out a bottle labelled POISON FOR RATS and poured the lot into the cake mixture!

When the poisoned cake was baked, she carried it up to Jack and gave it to him. When she had gone Jack looked at his cake and smiled with gratitude. Just then a bird tapped on the window with its beak. Jack turned suddenly and knocked the cake over. To his horror it splattered all over the floor.

"I'd better clean it all up and pretend that I ate it, or Hester Wallow will be cross with me. Oh, dear, what a pity, I would have so enjoyed it."

The bird on the windowsill looked at him, nodded his feathered head and flew away. It was as though it knew it had to save Jack's life!

Jack had just managed to clear up the mess of the chocolate cake when he heard someone coming up the stairs.

"Oh, dear, it must be Hester Wallow coming to

see if I've enjoyed my cake. I'll tell her I ate it and it was wonderful."

But it wasn't Hester Wallow, it was a strange and hideous looking woman! She seemed very tall as she stood in the doorway. Her hair was a wild tangled mess, she wore a large black cloak and when she spoke she had a sinister croaking voice. Jack was sure she was a witch and he leapt into bed pulling the bedcovers up under his chin.

"Hello, little dearie, I've come to tell you a bedtime story."

The peculiar woman told him a horrible story about a vampire who sucked blood from little boys. Poor Jack was terrified. Then the cloaked creature laughed and Jack realised it was his Aunt Selina wearing one of her wigs – a large black one.

"Please go away, Aunt Selina, you are frightening me."

"Don't be stupid, Jack, it's only a little joke. Where's your sense of humour? I've got an even better story for you, about a little boy who gets carried off and torn to pieces by a giant vulture."

While Aunt Selina was terrorising Jack, Hester Wallow crept up the stairs to find out if he was still alive. She heard a voice, and not knowing that Aunt Selina was in the room thought that it was Jack talking to himself.

"The dratted little nuisance is still alive," Hester muttered. "I'll bring up my polish and polish the top stair so much that it will be slippery and he will slip down the stairs and break his neck. Then Selina Allgood will reward me with a lot of money."

Wicked Hester Wallow did this and then crept away, just before Jack's Aunt

Selina came laughing out of Jack's room. Next moment the laughing stopped. There was the sound of someone sliding, a screech, and a lot of bumps as Aunt Selina went tumbling down the stairs.

She had to spend a week in bed with a bottle of gin and a bandage on her head. Every so often, she was heard mumbling, "I'll get him yet. I'll get the little snake. I'll finish him off."

Chapter 6

Jack Plans a Surprise

Jack was worried and nervous. By Friday he had to have the whole telephone directory copied out. It was pointless to ask his cousins to help him. He couldn't imagine why he had been so silly as to have asked them in the first place. His handwriting was quite good but he was slow. He kept noticing that the writing at the beginning of the page was neat and tidy, but by the time he had got halfway down, it had begun to wobble all over the place.

Looking out of his attic window, he saw that the sky was blue and the sun was shining. He decided to go out and have little walk around his island to cheer himself up.

It was cold outside but the air smelt of trees and plants and animals. There were still some bushes flowering in bright reds and yellows. Jack was glad that his cousins preferred lolling around in

front of the television set. At least
out of doors he could be free from
their constant nagging and criticism.
He went to an old oak tree that he
loved. He had made himself a
tree house in it. No one, only Jack,
knew of its existence.

Climbing into his tree house,
Jack pulled some crumbs from his
pocket and waited quietly. If
he was very still and quiet a
bird or squirrel usually came

to him. Today a bright-eyed squirrel hopped on to the branch near him.

"Hello, little squirrel. I have some crumbs for you." Cautiously the squirrel approached and looked enquiringly at Jack, then at the crumbs. Using both delicate black paws the squirrel picked up a crumb and sniffed it. Obviously the squirrel was not afraid of Jack, and soon he had eaten all the crumbs and hopped away again.

After that Jack went down to his cave. Since his cousins had arrived, Jack had spent more and more time there. Besides making dinosaur models in his room, he had also made some dinosaur puppets in the cave and now had a very good puppet family. He had even made a puppet theatre. The floor of the stage was covered with

sand and some seaweed; it was Jack's idea of the world before time began. Often he talked to his puppets, and by pulling pieces of string attached to their bodies could make them move.

There was a family of Tyrannosaurus and a family of Triceratops. Picking up the baby Triceratops, Jack said, "Why don't any of them like me? How can I get the family to like me?"

He knew that the puppets could not answer him back, but he still liked to chat to them. Then an idea came into his head. "Why don't I stage a puppet show for Marlene's birthday?" he thought. "It will be a surprise and then they will like me." He was so excited by the idea that he gave the baby dinosaur a kiss.

Then Jack decided that he had better have a rehearsal of his show and was so busy setting up his puppets that he did not notice a family of crabs who had crept into the cave and appeared to be watching him. They were very interested and when the play was over scurried out of the cave and off across the sand; the sound they made was just like people clapping – Jack was delighted.

"I'd better take the puppets and theatre straight up to the attic, then I can carry on rehearsing," Jack said aloud as he packed everything up.

The sun had disappeared and it had started raining; Jack had to carry his puppets and puppet theatre up to the house and it took him longer than usual to make the journey from the cave to the attic. When he had put the things away in his cupboard, he decided to go straight down to the dining room. He was afraid of being late for lunch.

The butler was laying the table. He frowned when he saw Jack.

"How dare you go sneaking out by yourself, then drag your dirty wet feet all over my floor!

From now on, your aunt has given strict orders that you will eat leftovers from the table, up in your attic. I shall bring them up myself," he added as though he was doing Jack a favour.

Jack was puzzled. "Why do I have to have leftovers? Why can't I eat with the family?"

"It's your aunt's orders| – |that's why. And if you've any sense, you'll know better than to disobey. Go on, off with you!"

Back in his attic, Jack felt very sad. Now he wasn't even allowed to eat with the family! It was so unfair. Why did Aunt Selina so hate him? Then he cheered up a bit when he thought of how pleased with him everyone would be when they saw the puppet show.

"Aunt Selina will let me come back to the dining room to eat when she sees the puppets."

Then he thought he had better copy some more names and addresses from the telephone directory, but he soon realised that he was running out of paper, so he went to the schoolroom to ask Ernest Croachbody for more.

The teacher was having his lunch, a pork pie and a bottle of beer. He looked very pleased with himself.

"The best pork pie I have tasted for a long time," he said, scoffing the last of it in one wolfish gulp.

"I need a lot more paper to copy out the telephone directory, Mr Croachbody. Could I have some, please?" Jack was always polite, no matter how difficult the circumstances.

Going to the cupboard, the teacher opened it and peered inside.

"I don't seem to have any. Supplies are not being delivered to the island until next week. That means you will have a week longer for your task."

"That's when Marlene is having her birthday party!" Jack's eyes were shining with delight. "I can hardly wait for the party, I love parties. *And* I have a surprise for Marlene on her birthday."

Ernest Croachbody smiled his big nasty smile. "*You* won't be going to any party, Jack, unless you have finished copying out the *whole* telephone directory."

Chapter 7

The Swimming Lesson

Next day was fine and warm and Aunt Selina decided that the children should have a swimming lesson in the lake in front of Allgood House. She had not forgotten that Jack had said that all the children should be able to swim, and she was terrified that her precious Wayne might drown. The butler was to give the lesson.

"Bring Jack down," she said to George Pomfret. "You can teach him as well."

Because no one ever paid any proper attention to Jack no one knew that he was a very powerful swimmer. Often he swam in the sea around the island.

There was a bright red and orange lifebelt for each child to wear in the water.

"Mine's better than yours," said Wayne to Jason.

"I'll learn to swim sooner than you," Jason told Wayne.

Marlene and Sharon thought they looked very attractive in their pink swimming suits and were showing off.

"*We* hope you'll both drown," Sharon told her brothers.

"Then you'll miss my party on Saturday," said Marlene viciously.

The children were always horrible and spiteful to each other. Their mother thought this was quite normal.

George Pomfret tied a piece of rope to each lifebelt and pulled each child along in the water, while Ernest Croachbody gave instructions.

"Paddle your hands and feet! One, two, one, two. ONE, TWO." He was marching up and down and getting in George Pomfret's way. "That's right. That's the way we did it in the army. Come on, now." He was bawling louder and louder as though he were on the army parade ground.

The exercise was too much for the fat, lazy butler, who began sweating and panting. Jack was sitting on the bank watching them. Aunt Selina kept jumping up and down, screaming.

"Be careful! Be careful! The children will drown."

Naturally, this made the children very nervous, so the swimming lesson was not a great success.

When it came to Jack's turn she smiled at him, a big bright smile.

"Put this lifebelt on, Jack. See what pretty colours it has? Lovely red and orange."

Jack didn't need a lifebelt, but he put it on to please his Aunt Selina. It felt unusually heavy, as though it was filled with weights.

He was puzzled, for he knew that a lifebelt should be as light as a feather.

"It's very heavy," he remarked.

"All the better to hold on to, Jack," she smiled. Turning to the butler, she spoke briskly. "I want you to take the boat out into the middle of the lake and leave Jack there. He can swim to the bank and we can all watch him. It will be such fun for all of us to see Jack learning to swim. And just think, Jack! As you are struggling – I mean, swimming – to the bank, we shall all be cheering like mad."

They all sat on the edge of the bank and watched as George Pomfret rowed right out into the middle of the lake. It was the deepest part of the lake. Shipping his oars, he made Jack stand up, then pushed him over the edge and quickly rowed back.

The first thing Jack felt was the weight of the lifebelt dragging him into the water. How curious, he thought to himself, it should make me more buoyant. He could see them all watching him and desperately wanted Aunt Selina to be proud of him and praise him. Determinedly he kicked his legs and started to breaststroke to the bank. It was very difficult, but although Jack was small, he was strong and wiry and could just about manage to swim with the heavy belt around his waist.

Unfortunately some water weeds got tangled around his legs. He remembered the golden rule that had helped him save Wayne's life – DON'T PANIC. He knew that if he kicked and struggled it would only make matters worse. So he stayed as still as possible, paddling the water with his hands until he felt the treacherous weeds uncurling from his legs.

Then with a tremendous effort of will and physical strength he started to swim to the edge of the lake. By the time he put his hands on the firm springy turf he was almost out of breath, but he clung on. Slowly he hauled himself from the water and flopped gratefully on to the grass.

Aunt Selina ran forward. Jack was sure she was going to praise him for his great effort; but she did not look at all pleased.

"So! He can swim! I should have known! All toads can swim!"

Taking the lifebelt from him, she threw it out into the middle of the lake. Jack was too out of breath and exhausted to look around but if he had cared to do so he would have seen that the brightly coloured lifebelt stayed on the surface of the water for one bare second, then sank straight to the bottom!

Chapter 8

The Puppet Show

Aunt Selina and her children were in the television room watching television. Every so often one of them would take the remote control and fiddle about with it.

Marlene and Sharon were watching their favourite programme about young people in Australia. Whenever a handsome boy came on to the screen, Marlene and Sharon would make funny cooing noises. This annoyed Jason and Wayne and whenever they thought their sisters were really interested in the programme they would flick over to another channel.

"Why don't you go and wash your hair in the toilet?" shrieked Marlene at Jason. "Leave us in peace to watch our programme!"

"It's junk, drivel. The stupidest programme I ever saw. Why can't we watch cartoons?"

Their mother, who had had quite a few gin and

tonics, was dozing on the sofa. Now she woke up.

"Children, children! Please stop that racket. My poor head aches. I've had the most exhausting day ringing up my friends to invite them to your birthday party."

"It's not fair, Mummy. Jason keeps tuning to another channel and we want to watch this Australian programme. It's our favourite – and it's educational."

Whenever the children's mother heard the word educational, her ears pricked up and her nose twitched, like a rat who smells grain.

"Oh, well, if it's educational, you had better watch it."

It was just as well that the only time Jack was allowed in to watch television was when the weather report was shown, otherwise he would probably have been blamed for the rows his cousins caused. Jack was not worried about

74

the television, anyway. He much preferred reading a book or exploring the island.

Ernest Croachbody, who was crouching on the floor beside the sofa, ready to pour the children's mother another drink, spoke. "Jack mentioned that he had some surprise for dear Marlene's birthday. I wonder what it can be?"

Aunt Selina frowned and sat up. "Surprise? Jack? That sounds a bit secretive. I don't think I like the sound of it."

"He probably wants to spoil my party," said Marlene. "Well, he's not coming, so there!"

Her mother looked concerned. "Of course the little rat won't spoil your party, darling. Heavens, Mr Croachbody, don't say he's turning out to be sly and secretive on top of everything else. I don't think I could stand it."

The butler had just come into the room with a tray of lemonade and biscuits for the children. They knocked each other over to get at the tray.

Their mother smiled fondly. "Just look at the little pets, they are so excited. Pomfret, bring Jack down. We had better ferret this secret out of him, or he might wreck the party."

Soon Jack was in the room and sat down thinking that he could watch television. There were no biscuits or lemonade left for him.

"Get up, Jack, you cheeky boy. Stop lolling around in that chair. I want to speak to you. Mr Croachbody says that you have some sly secret about Marlene's birthday party. Out with it! If you are planning to spoil her day you've got a nasty shock coming to you."

Jack smiled eagerly at his aunt. "Oh, no, Aunt Selina. I've got the most wonderful surprise for Marlene, for everybody. It's my own present to Marlene."

The children stopped quarelling and gathered around Jack.

"A present? For me? Give it to me – I love presents." Marlene spoke roughly.

Jack thought for a moment. "Well, it's supposed to be a surprise. If I tell you about it now, then it will spoil it for your birthday."

Marlene stamped her foot and her face went red. "Give it to me *now*."

"I bet he hasn't got anything, he just made it all up to make himself sound important," Jason jeered.

Give IT To Me NOW!

"I'm *not* making it up. It's true I *have* got a surprise, only it's not the sort of thing you can give."

"If it's not the sort of thing you can give, then how come it's a present?" said Sharon rudely.

Jack didn't want to give away the surprise but he saw that unless he told them, no one would believe him. So he said:

"I've made some puppets and a puppet theatre, and on the day of the party I'm going to give a performance to entertain everybody."

The children looked interested and Jack was delighted. Ernest Croachbody exchanged looks with Jack's aunt.

"What's all this nonsense?" said Aunt Selina impatiently. "*You* can't do anything, you have no brains! You had better show us this nonsense now, in case it turns out to be the rubbish I think it probably is. It will be better than having you make fools of us all in front of my important guests."

Jack ran from the room to get his dinosaur puppets, determined to prove to Aunt Selina that she was wrong. Soon he was back and setting up

78

his puppet theatre. It was quite a large stage, about a metre long and half a metre wide. It even had some little curtains. For lighting he had propped his torch behind the leaves and twigs he had made the bushes from. The effect was very realistic.

Dinosaurs →

Then he proudly took the dinosaurs from the box and arranged them on the sand-strewn stage.

Making friends ←

It was a very simple play about two families of dinosaurs who were always fighting. But then the baby dinosaurs of each family made friends with each other and ended the fighting.

The children were enthralled and could not help but show how interested they were. Mr Croachbody nodded surprised approval at Jack.

"I didn't know he had it in him," he muttered.

Jack heard him and was so happy that he nearly burst.

"It's quite impressive, Jack," said Aunt Selina. "Where did you get those dinosaurs? Did you steal them?"

"No, I made them all by myself."

"How did you make them?" asked Jason.

Jack explained that he had collected all sorts of materials from the beach and with the help of his little pocket knife had carved each piece. Then he had used glue to stick them together.

"It would be fabulous for my birthday party, Jack," said Marlene. "You must show them. Mummy, tell Jack he has to show the puppets on my birthday."

"If that's what you want, darling. Actually, they are very clever and realistic."

Jack thought he would burst with pride and happiness. At last! His family approved of him. He smiled so happily at them that he thought he could never stop smiling.

Then Wayne started a rumpus. Wayne hated to

see Jack the centre of attention. He was used to being his mother's pet. Also he was peeved that *he* had not thought of the puppet idea. It was Jack who had thought of that – and Jack was a whole year younger than he was!

All Wayne ever did was to sit in front of the television set. He never knew how to make anything because he was too lazy to try. The only use he put his hands to was to stuff his mouth with sweets, crisps and burgers. But Wayne had learned a very nasty trick to get sympathy and attention. He discovered that if he crammed his hands into his mouth, it made him choke and look ill, and brought tears into his eyes. He shoved his hands into his mouth and choking and gasping staggered to his mother's lap.

"Mummy, Mummy!" he cried out in his babyish voice. "I feel sick."

His mother clasped her arms around him and looked with horror at her sobbing, retching child.

"My own darling! What is it? Tell mummy, darling. Let her help you, my precious."

"It's those nasty dinosaurs, I'm frightened of them. Make Jack take them away."

Instantly Aunt Selina leapt to her feet and charged at Jack like a maddened bull.

"You horror! Take those dreadful things away.

Wayne is perfectly right. I believe you only brought them here to scare my baby. You should be ashamed of yourself, terrorising an innocent child." She kicked the dinosaur models around so that they broke and scattered.

Her innocent child was smirking at Jack behind his mother's back, and when he thought no one was looking deliberately trod on the baby Triceratops.

Jack picked up the broken dinosaurs, and cradled the baby Triceratops sadly.

He had spent so many loving hours of labour on these models and Aunt Selina had broken them in a minute. She must have been terribly upset about Wayne and that made her lose her temper, he decided. She *couldn't* have been so unkind as to smash his precious dinosaurs up deliberately. It would take hours to repair them, but he decided that he would do it.

"I didn't come down to frighten Wayne, Aunt Selina. I shall go away now and repair my dinosaurs."

"I don't care what you do with them, just keep them away from my children. We certainly don't want them at the party. For that matter we don't want *you* at the party either. Goodness knows what you'd get up to!"

Chapter 9

Jack is Punished

It was the Wednesday before the party. Jack was getting very hungry. The table scraps had not amounted to much in the past few days and Hester Wallow had taken to locking up the kitchen since last week when Jack had gone down to make himself some supper.

Jack thought that George Pomfret and the housekeeper would be in their own sitting room watching television, and planned to make an omelette. Just as he was opening the refrigerator to take out some eggs, he heard the sounds of the butler and housekeeper in the passage outside. Quickly he hid in the room behind the range.

"I hope they hurry up and leave," he thought. "Otherwise I shall starve."

Then he thought that he would play his ghost noise trick again and scare them away. Taking a deep breath, he made a terrific screeching and

wailing noise into the chimney. It was a dreadful sound, like a vampire gone mad with toothache. Then he tried to make the noise again but he laughed so much that he couldn't. Cautiously he crept back to the kitchen door and peered through the keyhole. George Pomfret and Hester Wallow were jammed in the doorway leading out of the kitchen, pushing and scrabbling at each other, looking demented with fear.

As soon as they had gone, Jack made his omelette and went off to bed contented and happy. But Hester Wallow always locked the kitchen after that and Aunt Selina forbade everyone to go near the place after dark.

Jack wished he had a key to the kitchen, but as he hadn't he just had to wait for George Pomfret to bring up his scraps. He was still copying out the telephone directory and now put down his pen and rubbed his chilled fingers. Then he heard slow, heavy footsteps on the stairs.

"Good! That will be the butler with my scraps. I hope there is more than yesterday. I'm really hungry now," thought Jack.

Slowly the door opened and George Pomfret's big fat sagging body was framed in the doorway.

Jack was so hungry that for once he forgot his manners. "Give me my food, I'm starving."

The butler looked annoyed. "Manners, man-

ners. How about a please and thank you?"

"Give me my food, you silly man," Jack shouted, beginning to lose his temper.

"This is a fine way to carry on when I have kindly toiled all the way up here with your scraps!"

Now Jack was really angry. "Give me my food at once, or I'll *really* call you names you won't want to hear. You'r _ a big cissy to run away from the kitchen ghost. *Now* – GIVE ME MY FOOD!"

George Pomfret's face quivered with rage.

"That's no way to talk to your elders and betters, you horrible child. I see a lesson is in order."

Going to the window and opening it, the butler tipped the contents of the plate out.

"*That's* the reward you get for your bad manners. I shall go down and tell your aunt that you are turning into a right little savage."

"I'm *not* a savage," said Jack angrily. "I'm hungry and you are a cruel, wicked man to throw my food away."

"I did it for your own good. Next time you will remember to say please. I shall have to report this to your aunt, and see what she has to say. I don't for an instant think she will want such a bad-tempered little savage at Marlene's birthday party."

As soon as the butler had gone downstairs, Jack decided that he would go to the beach and fish for his supper. He had done it many a time in the past when his parents had been alive. It was something he was used to.

It was a dark overcast day, one of those days when everything looks lonely as though the world would be happier asleep. Jack soon caught a fish and took it to his cave. He lit a fire and when it was blazing and giving out some heat, he took the frying pan that was kept in the cave and put the fish on to cook. It didn't take long and Jack was so hungry that he didn't bother getting out his knife and fork, but ate with his fingers. It was

the best dinner he had had for a long time and he enjoyed every scrap.

So busy was he with his cooking and eating that Jack didn't notice it had started to rain until he took his pan out to clean it. Rubbing sand into it, he took the pan to the water's edge and swilled water around it to rinse it.

Then he set off for Allgood House in the pouring rain.

Finding his secret path was too slippery and muddy, he hurried down the beach to the path he used in earlier times and started to climb up. Glancing up, he thought he saw George Pomfret and Hester Wallow standing on the cliff at the head of the path.

"I must be imagining things," he told himself. "It's getting dark, and I've made a mistake. They never go out in the rain."

Grasping a tree root he hauled himself up the path and was about halfway up when a sound alerted him. Looking up he saw to his absolute horror a huge boulder come tumbling down the cliff – straight at him! He would certainly be killed if it hit! With the speed of light Jack leapt nimbly to one side as the boulder hurtled past him and crashed noisily to the beach below.

So shocked and frightened was Jack that he almost slithered back down the path to join the

boulder on the beach, but somehow he managed to find the strength to climb to the top. There was no one in sight.

"It's so long since I've used this path that I didn't realise that there was a boulder there," thought Jack. "The rain must have loosened it and made it roll down the cliff. I've had a very lucky escape from a terrible death!"

Jack was wearing thin clothes – they were all he had. Now they were badly torn and looked like rags. By the time he got to his attic he was shivering and sneezing.

Climbing into bed he pulled his blankets over him. They warmed him slightly, but he was worried.

"Oh dear! Atichoo! Atichoo! I think I'm getting a cold and if I have a cold I won't be able to do my work tomorrow. If I can't do my work, I won't be able to go to the party. Whatever am I going to do?"

Chapter 10

Jack and the Rats

By the next morning Jack's head was throbbing, his throat was sore, he was terribly thirsty, he had a temperature and his thin body was racked with pain.

"I feel so ill I cannot get out of bed," he said aloud. "When my food is sent up, I'll ask the butler to send for my aunt. She will nurse me back to health and take off these damp rags and give me some dry warm clothes."

All day Jack stayed in bed and sometimes he dozed and sometimes he lay awake looking at the ceiling pretending that his mother was still alive and talking to him in her soft gentle voice. Once he cried, and felt hot tears run down his scorching cheeks. Having a cold is a wretched business and makes a person inclined to cry for no real reason.

Eventually he heard George Pomfret's heavy

footsteps coming up the stairs. He would even be glad to see the butler's miserable face, he felt so depressed. The footsteps stopped outside the door.

"I'm leaving your food out here. I'm not coming into your room because you are so rude and bad-tempered."

Jack tried to call out, but his throat was so sore that he could only whisper, "Help me." But the butler did not hear him.

Jack was too ill to get out of bed to get his food. In any case, he didn't have any appetite, he was just thirsty and wanted a drink.

Then Jack cheered up as he thought to himself that when the butler next came upstairs he would see that the food had not been touched and must surely come into the room to see if anything was wrong.

Jack heard the footsteps coming up the stairs again the following day, and his hopes rose. He heard the butler approaching the door. He could have cried with disappointment when the footsteps stopped and the door did not open.

"I see that you have left your food," George Pomfret shouted irritably. "You are probably sulking, you ungrateful boy. Well, I'm taking away yesterday's plate and leaving you another plate. But mind you eat it!"

Making a supreme effort, Jack called out, "I'm

ill, Mr Pomfret. Can you hear me? I'm ill. Ask my aunt to come up and see me."

There was a pause.

"Are you sure you're not play-acting? Your aunt said you were a liar."

Jack called out in his strongest voice. "I *am* ill. Tell her to come at once."

When the butler had gone Jack heard a sound he knew and dreaded.

It was the scurrying of rats!

They were not in his room, they were outside the door. Then he heard the chink of a plate and guessed that the rats were eating his dinner.

Soon there was a lighter tread on the stairs.

"It must be Aunt Selina!" Jack was delighted and realised how badly he needed to see someone to talk to and tell how much he had suffered with his bad cold.

But the voice on the other side of the door was not the voice of Aunt Selina. It was a voice Jack

knew, and hated. It was the sharp angry rasp of Hester Wallow, the spiteful housekeeper. "Why! You've eaten everything. You've cleared your plate. There's nothing wrong with you at all. Just as I thought! Play-acting!" Jack tried to call out, but he had a fit of coughing and could not explain to her that the rats had eaten his dinner.

"And you can stop that phony coughing. I know you are putting it on to be dramatic. A boy who can eat is not ill."

There is nothing worse in the world than being told that if you can eat you are not ill. It's perfectly possible to feel dreadful and still fancy a sweet or a biscuit. In Jack's case he hadn't eaten anything at all.

As his coughing fit died away he heard Hester Wallow's feet tip-tapping down the stairs and could imagine her thin face with the downturned mouth and long carrot-like nose.

"If only Aunt Selina would come," he said
sadly. "She would rescue me, for I am dreadfully
ill and wretchedly unhappy."

face He could IMaGiNe her thin
With the doWN turNed Mouth and
LoNG caRRoT Nose

Chapter 11

Marlene's Party

It was the day of Marlene's birthday party. Jack's fever had gone and he no longer had the terrible headache. Colds have to run their course. But he was weak and hungry. All day he heard the whirring and purring of engines as boats and planes arrived on the island for the party.

"They will come for me soon. I know they could not be so cruel as to leave me in an attic when there is a big party downstairs. I am too weak to get up, or I would go down by myself," said poor Jack to the ceiling of his lonely room.

Downstairs all was bustle and excitement. The house was full of light and colour. Marlene wore her best outfit and her mother had allowed her to wear some make-up now that she was a teenager. Sharon was very jealous of this because she wasn't allowed to wear make-up.

"You look horrible," she told Marlene in a

sneering voice. "You look like a big painted pig."

Marlene was admiring herself in the mirror, thinking how gorgeous she was and how everyone would stare at her in admiration.

"Even if you did wear make-up, Sharon, it wouldn't stop you looking like a pasty little ferret. So, shut up!"

There were presents everywhere. The tables were piled high with food, the most delicious food anyone had ever seen.

Trays of little sausages, gleaming and steaming. Dishes as big as saucepans were filled with crisps. There were huge bowls of popcorn of different colours. There was a whole tray filled with chipsticks and another filled with cheese straws. On one round table was a massive circular plate on which a great red jelly wobbled. On another table was a big pink blancmange with hundreds and thousands scattered all over it like jewels. There was the biggest and thickest chocolate cake ever seen, with chocolate and cream oozing down the sides. On the sideboard there were twenty-seven different varieties of ice cream.

Marlene kept dipping her fingers into it, until Hester Wallow told her not to make a show of herself in front of the guests.

Buckets of fizzy drink had been placed around the room with trays of cups nearby. Jason and Sharon almost fell into one of the buckets, so greedily were they hogging lemonade. A tray loaded with sandwiches was placed on a table near the door and as people came in they took a sandwich, then a drink from George Pomfret.

An endless stream of children and adults all came through the front door, dressed in their best

clothes and looking very smart. Soon there were
a hundred people in the drawing room of Allgood
House.

George Pomfret was wearing his best black suit
with a white shirt, and looked grander than any
of the guests. Hester Wallow smiled a lot, even
though her face wasn't built for smiling. Everyone forgot about Jack.

The children and their parents were all friends
of Aunt Selina and they didn't even know that
Jack existed. They were all having a wonderful
time, stuffing food into their faces, pulling crack-
ers and laughing at silly jokes.

There was an almighty banging on the front door.

"Don't let anyone else in, Pomfret," said Aunt Selina. "There are no more guests expected. It's probably some upstart like the ferryman thinking he can barge his way into free goodies at my expense. They are all at it, you know," she said to the adults, "all taking advantage of my goodness and generosity since I came into all this money."

"Dear, sweet, kind Selina," the guests said over and over again. "So beautiful, so kind." Aunt Selina loved every minute of it, and couldn't make up her mind whether to look saintly and sweet or very beautiful.

No one guessed for a minute that she had a nephew to whom she was cruel and wicked, and that at the very minute they were praising her, he was lying on his bed wishing he could be at the party.

The banging on the front door grew louder and louder. Gradually everyone stopped talking and listened. One by one the children and adults began to drift into the hall. The banging was so loud that Aunt Selina was afraid that the front door might be knocked down.

"You had better open it, Pomfret," she said at last.

"Very well, madam." George Pomfret went to the front door in his stateliest manner, aware that everyone was watching him. Determined to show all the fine guests that he knew just how the perfect butler should behave, he walked in a very grand way.

Unfortunately he looked like an over-sized ballerina, and several people smiled behind their hands, as they always do when a person shows off.

Over-sized Ballerina

Opening the door he prepared to be very dignified and firm with the intruder.

On the doorstep was the biggest woman anyone had ever seen. She was as tall as George Pomfret or Ernest Croachbody. Her face was so lined that she seemed very old. Her eyes were small and bright, like a very alert bird. She wore black from head to toe and at her throat she had a great shiny diamond brooch. In one hand she carried a large walking stick. A green and red parrot sat on her shoulder.

George Pomfret looked her over from head to toe, he ignored the parrot. The butler was haughty and proud.

"I am sorry, madam, this is a private party. You cannot come in."

The old lady cackled with laughter and lashed out at him with her stick.

"I've just come from the Amazon and I eat people like you for breakfast. So, push off, windbag!" She had a very strong American accent.

Everyone stared at her in surprise. She was the strangest sight they had ever seen.

"Where's Selina Allgood?" demanded the old lady.

"Selina Allgood," cried the parrot in a raucous voice.

When the old lady walked into the house and everyone carried on staring at her with interest and surprise, she didn't seem to mind at all. She stared back at the finely dressed guests, the presents, the food and finally at the birthday cake with thirteen candles.

"Good heavens!" said Aunt Selina faintly. "It's Aunt Marigold from America. I thought you died years ago exploring the Amazon."

Aunt Marigold laughed out loud.

"No, sir! I'm very much alive. You can't kill

an Allgood that easily. Still swilling gin, I see, Selina."

"Swilling gin," repeated the parrot, and everyone laughed.

"Aunt Marigold is so droll," said Aunt Selina. "She is our dear aunt and we are all so fond of her."

She went to kiss Aunt Marigold, but the parrot pecked her on the nose and she jumped back with a cry of alarm.

"Go up and have a nice lie down, Aunt Marigold. I am sure you must be very tired after your long journey from the Amazon."

"Don't be stupid, Selina. I'm never tired. No American woman ever admits to being tired, it's a sign of old age. No American woman ever grows old. Give me some food and drink and then let me see the children."

Marlene came up to her. "Who is this peculiar old woman? I want that parrot for a birthday present. Mother, tell this silly old woman that I want that parrot. She's got to give him to me."

Selina Allgood smiled, she could put on a very charming act when she chose.

"I am sure that Aunt Marigold will give you Polly. The dear old lady has a very kind heart."

Aunt Marigold snorted.

"The dear old lady has no heart when little girls

108

are rude to her, and my parrot's name is *not* Polly, it is Mr Exparden. Mr Exparden is mine, he's my friend and I'm not giving him to you."

Marlene started whingeing and crying. Her mother was upset.

"Now look what you've done. You've made her cry," she said reproachfully to Aunt Marigold.

"Good!" said Aunt Marigold.

"Good!" said Mr Exparden, the parrot.

"Now, I want to see the children," said Aunt Marigold.

Jason, Wayne, Marlene and Sharon were brought forward to shake hands with Aunt Marigold. They did this very prettily because

Ernest Croachbody had been teaching them all week how to do it and now he was standing over them, watching.

Aunt Marigold sat down. "Very nice, Selina." Then she peered around the room.

Jack's aunt looked uneasily at Ernest Croachbody, George Pomfret and Hester Wallow.

Aunt Marigold tapped her stick on the floor and rapped out suddenly and loudly, "Where's Jack?"

"Where's Jack?" repeated Mr Exparden.

"Well, Selina?" repeated Aunt Marigold. "Where's Jack?"

Chapter 12

Jack Finds a Friend

The attic was cold and Jack was miserable.

"I'm fed up lying here, hoping that someone will come for me. They won't come now."

He had heard the sounds of a very good party in progress downstairs and wished that he could go, but realised he had no decent clothes to wear.

"I'll have to do something about this," he said to himself. "Otherwise, no one will help me."

Climbing out of bed, he went over to the cupboard where he kept some of his dinosaur models. Opening it he took out the baby Triceratops. They had all been repaired, it had taken a whole week, but the result made him very proud of himself and his abilities.

"What shall I do?" he asked the dinosaur.

The dinosaur stared back at him with large round eyes; Jack thought that the dinosaur would have said, if he could have talked, "Run away".

"But where can I run to?" Jack was sad. "I have nobody." Then for some strange reason he remembered the moment on the beach when his parents had given him the dinosaur book for his birthday and told him another story about his Aunt Marigold.

"Daddy said that Aunt Marigold must be dead. But Mum said that she might be alive. I know what I'll do! I'll escape from here and try to find Aunt Marigold in the Amazon!"

Immediately Jack felt a lot better.

"If I try to go out of the front door someone will try to stop me and then I'll never get away."

He knew that there were a lot of planes and boats parked and moored around the island. If he could escape he could hide on one of them and get away from the island. But how to escape from the house without being seen?

"I'll tie my sheets and blankets together and make a rope and climb out of the window!"

In no time at all he had made a very good rope and was climbing down it. It was very hard work; he was weak and if he fell it was a long way to the ground. But it would all be worth it. Jack was fed up with the way he had been treated and wanted to put things right. He was determined that he was going to try to find his Aunt Marigold.

"I am leaving Allgood House and shall not return until I find my Aunt Marigold."

About halfway down he heard a peculiar noise. It was like a soft scratching sound; then there was a very faint "cheep, cheep".

"That sounds like a bird in trouble," thought Jack. "But where could the sound be coming from?" He looked upwards and saw a tiny sparrow perched on his windowsill. One wing was tucked in but the other was spread out awkwardly. Jack desperately wanted to escape from Allgood House and find his Aunt Marigold, but a creature of the wild was injured and needed him.

"Don't worry, sparrow, I'm coming to help you," he called softly, and began the slow laborious climb back up the rope.

Back in his room, Jack lifted the injured sparrow very gently from the windowsill to the table. He could feel its heart beating rapidly. It did not take long to mend the injured wing; then Jack put the bird into a shoe box and covered it with an old pullover. In a couple of days' time the bird would be ready to fly again. Then Jack had a thought.

"Oh, dear, if I go away now, then who will look after you, sparrow? I shall have to stay a little while longer."

In any case, the effort of climbing first down, then back up had exhausted Jack who felt dizzy and collapsed on to his bed.

Chapter 13

Where's Jack?

Downstairs Aunt Selina was in a terrible state.

"I'm afraid dear Aunt Marigold is really very tired after her long journey and really must rest. I am going to insist that George Pomfret, Hester Wallow and Ernest Croachbody carry her up to bed this very instant." Aunt Selina spoke kindly but firmly. She had looked around at her guests with her eyebrows raised, as much as to say, "We've had enough of this old crackpot".

The guests all looked on with amusement as the teacher, the butler and the housekeeper all tried to shift Aunt Marigold. Aunt Marigold had once floored an elephant and wrestled with an alligator, and it was child's play to push Hester Wallow so hard that she fell on her bottom. Then she jabbed George Pomfret in the stomach with her stick; he doubled up and ran away to hide behind a potted plant. Ernest Croachbody

came to her with his nasty wolfish smile. Aunt Marigold had learned to outstare a venomous snake, so she simply smiled back at the teacher, and as he crept forward, waited until he was within range of her stick. With the speed of light she jabbed the stick into his foot and laughed as he leapt back howling with pain and rage.

The guests had started talking in puzzled whispers, then the whispers got louder.

"The old lady is mad!"

"She should be locked up!"

"It's disgraceful treating poor Selina Allgood like this!"

"Selina Allgood only has four children. She *must* be mad to talk of someone called Jack. There is no Jack."

Aunt Selina could see they were all on her side and she walked up to Aunt Marigold.

116

"Why don't you let *me* take you upstairs? When you have had a good sleep, you'll forget all this Jack nonsense."

All the guests began murmuring, "Good idea, good idea."

Then Aunt Marigold stood up. She tapped her stick on the floor; Mr Exparden smoothed down his feathers and straightened himself up. His eyes were watchful. There was complete silence in the hall. Then she spoke.

"I didn't come here for Marlene's party. I came here to see my nephew's son, Jack. *And*, I'm not budging from this spot until I've seen him."

Quite suddenly Aunt Marigold had stopped appearing to be a silly old lady with strange habits. She was a terrifying figure of authority.

Everyone listened to her and everyone believed her.

Aunt Selina looked uneasy and a bit frightened. Wayne, who was standing beside her, had blown up a crisp bag and was about to pop it when his mother clouted him on the ear and didn't even notice when his face puckered up in his usual preparation for a bout of tears.

"Where's Jack?" said Aunt Marigold.

"Where's Jack?" said Mr Exparden.

"Where's Jack?" said all the guests.

Aunt Marigold looked at the housekeeper, who was still sitting on the floor,

and the butler, who was still hiding behind the potted plant. "Get up off your backside, lady. And, you, windbag, come out from your hiding place and fetch Jack to me this very instant!"

118

The butler and the housekeeper were both afraid of the strange American lady who might attack them again at any moment, and before Aunt Selina could stop them ran out of the hall and up the stairs to Jack's attic.

They found him lying on his bed, his face very pale, too weak to walk.

"Whatever are we going to do, Hester?" George Pomfret's face was as white as Jack's and he was sweating profusely. "He can't walk."

"We'll have to take him down on a stretcher. There is one in the back of the closet. If we don't get him down quickly, we'll have that Aunt Marigold down on us, and I can't take any more of it. Can you?"

"No. Right, Hester, let's put him on a stretcher and get straight down. We'll just say he's had a bit of a cold."

When the guests saw the thin, ragged little boy carried into the hall on a stretcher, they gasped with horror. The children stopped eating and looked up at their parents, who had expressions of the greatest dismay on their faces.

"Great heavens!" cried one woman who had been very friendly with Aunt Selina. "Is that Jack?" Then she stared at Aunt Selina, "Who *is* this, Selina?"

A man with a black jacket, with a red rose in his buttonhole, said, "Is it possible that this ragged child lives in *this* big posh mansion?"

A small woman with kind eyes said, "How could anyone treat a child like this?" and fainted into the arms of the man with the red rose in his buttonhole.

A little girl in a white frock walked up to the stretcher. There were tears in her eyes. "No child should be treated like this, it's terrible." Then the little girl looked at Jason, Wayne, Marlene and Sharon. "I think you are all horrible and cruel. How could you possibly be down here at this wonderful party, eating your heads off, when this poor boy is on a stretcher? I don't want any of you for friends."

"Who *is* he anyway?" asked a boy with curly hair. "What's he doing here?"

Aunt Selina had a guilty white face, and her children all ran to hide behind her; they, too, looked guilty and ashamed.

Aunt Marigold went up to the stretcher and took Jack's hand. There was a very tender look on her face. Even Mr Exparden, who was nodding his feathered head up and down, looked pityingly down at Jack.

Then Aunt Marigold looked around at the guests who were waiting with open mouths for her to speak.

"I flew straight here because I have just heard that my nephew has died. It takes a long time for letters to reach the Amazon. This is the son of my late nephew. His name is Jack Allgood. He owns this fine house, this island, houses all over the world, millions of pounds and fleets of ships and aeroplanes. He is one of the richest boys in the world. *He* is master here! And he has to be carried to this fine party on a stretcher!" She glared fiercely at Jack's Aunt Selina. "*That* woman was entrusted with care of this poor child. Does anyone here think that she has cared for him properly?" All the guests shook their heads. "Account for yourself, wicked woman!"

"Account for yourself!" said Mr Exparden.

"Account for yourself!" said all the guests.

Jack moaned feebly and tried to prop himself up on one elbow.

"It's all right, Aunt Marigold. It's not Aunt Selina's fault. I like living up in the attic. I couldn't come to the party because I was not able to finish copying out the telephone directory as my teacher, Mr Croachbody, told me to do. I couldn't finish it because I was very ill. Please, don't blame my Aunt Selina, she never comes to my attic any more since the time she came to tell me a story wearing a strange wig that frightened me very much. She explained that I was being silly and she was only playing a little joke on me. But she fell down the stairs because the housekeeper had put too much polish on the top step. That's why she didn't know I was ill. I caught a bad cold when I went fishing for my dinner."

The guests had all gasped with shock and looked quite horrified. They had begun staring at Aunt Selina as though she were a poisonous snake.

GuesTs Looking hoRRified →

"Fishing for your dinner?" Aunt Marigold was aghast. "What call can there be for an immensely rich boy to fish for his dinner?"

Now the guests began to look a bit guilty when they looked at the mountains of food they had been eating and then at the ragged child who had to fish for his own dinner.

"It's difficult to explain," said Jack. "I was rude to Mr Pomfret when he brought my scraps and leftovers from the table up to my attic –"

"She made me do it," blubbered the butler.

"Silence, windbag!" barked Aunt Marigold. "Carry on, Jack!"

"So, to teach me a lesson, he had to throw my scraps out of the window. I was very hungry, so I went down to the beach and caught a fish and cooked it. You would have been proud of me, Aunt Marigold."

Fierce old Aunt Marigold had tears in her eyes.

She squeezed Jack's hand. "I *am* proud of you, Jack."

"But on the way I caught a cold. No one believed I was ill because the rats ate my plate of scraps that were left outside my door." The guests, who were listening with fascinated horror, looked ill. Some had to press handkerchiefs over their mouths, many were openly crying. "Hester Wallow thought I was play-acting, because she thought I had eaten the scraps. Aunt Selina couldn't have known anything about it. I don't want you to blame her. I am sure if she had known about it, she would have come to rescue me."

By now the guests had all moved away from Aunt Selina and her children and were standing behind Jack. They gently patted his hands, their tears spilled down their faces.

"It's the most dreadful story I have ever heard," they said one to the other. "The woman must be a monster, and the children are no better."

A girl in a red spotted skirt came up to Marlene and told her: "I wish you a very *unhappy* birthday, Marlene, you beast."

Then everyone sang "Unhappy birthday to you, unhappy birthday, rotten Marlene, unhappy birthday to you."

"It's not my fault," cried Marlene.

"Oh, yes it is. It is all your faults, you are the most horrible people in the world." The children and their parents agreed with the girl in the red spotted skirt.

Aunt Marigold looked at Aunt Selina and shook her head sadly. "Such a beautiful face and such a wicked heart."

Then Aunt Marigold picked Jack up from the stretcher and held him up so that he could see everyone and they could see him. "This is the pluckiest little guy I've ever come across."

"Three cheers for Jack," shouted one of the grown-ups.

When they had all finished cheering Jack and smiling at his look of pure joy, they got on their coats.

"Don't go!" cried Aunt Selina. "I can explain everything. Please, stay."

"I wouldn't stay with you in a ratpit," said one man who had previously been admiring her.

All the guests left, muttering "*Such* a wicked woman, such *horrible* children. We'll never be friends with her again."

Then Aunt Marigold said: "You *are* horrible, Selina, and contemptible. To have such an evil heart is an awful thing. I am taking Jack away with me right now to the Amazon, for a little holiday. Would you like that, Jack?"

Jack was sorry that Marlene's party had been spoiled. Also he was sorry that everyone seemed to think everything was Aunt Selina's fault. But he already loved this strange Aunt Marigold and Mr Exparden and he couldn't wait to go to the Amazon. It had always sounded a really exciting place.

"I have a plane outside, Jack. Why don't we hop on it and fly straight to the Amazon, this very minute?"

Jack thought that sounded a wonderful idea.

"Good idea!" said Jack.

"Good idea!" squawked Mr Exparden.

"Let's go," said Aunt Marigold.

And off they all went for a wonderful holiday on the Amazon.